✚ Doll Hospital ✚

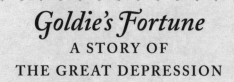

Goldie's Fortune
A STORY OF
THE GREAT DEPRESSION

Doll Hospital #1
Tatiana Comes to America
AN ELLIS ISLAND STORY

Doll Hospital #2
Goldie's Fortune
A STORY OF
THE GREAT DEPRESSION

Doll Hospital #3
Glory's Freedom
A STORY OF
THE UNDERGROUND RAILROAD

✚ Doll Hospital ✚

Goldie's Fortune

A STORY OF
THE GREAT DEPRESSION

BY JOAN HOLUB

Illustrations by Cheryl Kirk Noll

A LITTLE APPLE PAPERBACK

SCHOLASTIC INC.

New York Toronto London Auckland Sydney
Mexico City New Delhi Hong Kong Buenos Aires

No part of this publication may be reproduced
in whole or in part, or stored in a retrieval system,
or transmitted in any form or by any means,
electronic, mechanical, photocopying, recording, or
otherwise, without written permission of the publisher.
For information regarding permission, write to
Scholastic Inc., Attention: Permissions Department,
557 Broadway, New York, NY 10012.

ISBN 0-439-40179-8

Design by Steve Scott

12 11 10 9 8 7 6 5 4 3 2 1   2 3 4 5 6 7/0
                                          40

Printed in the U.S.A.
First Scholastic printing, October 2002

For Joy Peskin, who thought of doll hospitals.

*With thanks to my mom for taking me and
my doll Annie to a doll hospital.*
—J.H.

Table of Contents

1. Colorful Rags 1

2. Ick-o-rama 6

3. Super-weird 10

4. Dork Elementary 13

5. Good and Bad 19

6. Checkup 22

7. A One-of-a-Kind Doll 27

8. My Girl 31

9. Stuck-up 34

10. Trouble 38

11. Everything Goes 43

12. Empty 48

13. Poor Nana? 52

14. All Wet 57

15. The Dream Team 60

16. The Face Snatchers 62

17. Feeling Better 68

18. A Hard Life 72

19. The Pawnshop 76

20. Wishing 79

21. Money 83

22. Riches to Rags 85

23. A New Goldie 87

24. Now or Never 91

25. The Gift 94

26. Eliza 100

Glossary 103

Questions and Answers About the
Great Depression 105

✚ Doll Hospital ✚

Goldie's Fortune
A STORY OF
THE GREAT DEPRESSION

CHAPTER 1
✦ Colorful Rags ✦

Rose dug through her dresser drawers. "Where's my yellow hair thingie? The one Mom made for me." She stomped into the bathroom and glared at her little sister, Lila.

"I don't know, crab-face," said Lila. Her mouth was full of toothpaste suds. She was getting ready for the first day of school, too.

"Thanks a lot, bubble-gums," said Rose.

Lila grinned widely to show lots of foam. "Doctor came. What a shame. There are no maybes: I've got rabies!"

"Ha-ha! Very *not* funny." Rose stomped back to their room. Lila finished brushing her teeth and followed.

"At home I knew where everything was." Rose banged her jumbled drawers open and shut. "Here, everything is a big, fat mess. I can't find anything!"

Lila spotted Rose's yellow triangle-shaped knitted hair scarf under the dresser. She grabbed it by its two tie strings and handed it to Rose. "Here."

Rose frowned at it. Back at their old school in the city, she had worn the hair scarf a lot. But maybe she'd better not today. She didn't want to take the chance of looking too different from the other kids. She threw the scarf into her drawer and slammed it shut. "Never mind."

"Crab-head," Lila grumbled.

Rose didn't know why she was being so mean to Lila. It wasn't her fault they had to live with their grandmother. It wasn't her fault they had to go to a new school.

It was because their parents were in Africa for the year. They were doctors who specialized in treating rare diseases. The African villages where they were working weren't safe enough for Rose and Lila. So the girls had had to stay behind in America at their grandmother's in the very same house where their mom had grown up. They had golden lockets with their parents' pictures inside. But that and their parents' weekly phone calls were all they had left of their mom and dad for a whole year.

"Are we going to do cold lunch or hot?" asked Lila.

"Hot," said Rose. "I don't want to take a bag lunch until I see what the other kids bring."

"Then I guess you'll be buying lunch in the school crab-ateria," said Lila.

"You're *sooo* funny. Maybe you should eat in the laugh-ateria," said Rose. "By yourself."

"Let's see," Lila went on. "You could have crab apples for lunch. And crab cakes for dessert —"

"Well, you could have —" began Rose.

Ding-dong! The doorbell rang, cutting her off.

Rose and Lila looked out their bedroom window to see who it was.

Their room had been their mother's bedroom when she was a girl. It was on the second floor, around the corner from a turret on the third floor called the witch's hat.

The witch's hat had gotten its nickname because of its tall, pointed roof. It was where their grandmother had her doll hospital. People brought her old or broken dolls, and she fixed them. A few weeks ago, Rose and Lila had helped her fix a doll named Tatiana. Tatiana belonged to Nadia, a girl who was their neighbor.

"Somebody's on the front porch," said Rose. "I can only see feet. It looks like the person is hopping. Maybe it's that next-door girl, Nadia."

"Or maybe it's her doll, Tatiana, begging to come back," said Lila. "Maybe she hates living with Nadia and misses us."

"Tatiana is too short to reach the doorbell," said Rose.

"Well, maybe that's why she's hopping. If she stood on her tippy doll toes, and if she stretched her little doll fingers —" began Lila.

Ding-dong!

"Can you girls get that?" called their grandmother. She was way up in the witch's hat.

Rose and Lila raced downstairs, each trying to get to the door first.

Rose won. "Blue ribbon to me, thank you very much."

Their grandmother's door didn't have a peephole like their apartment door back home in the city. So they peeked out the tall, skinny window next to the front door.

It wasn't Nadia. Or Tatiana.

It was a woman holding a bundle of colorful rags. Her face was wrinkled, but she didn't act old. She was wearing a tracksuit, and she was jogging in place. Her gray-haired ponytail bounced up and down as she jogged.

Rose opened the door.

The woman stopping jogging. "Is this the doll hospital?"

Rose and Lila nodded.

The woman held out her rag bundle.

Only then Rose and Lila saw it wasn't rags. It was a doll!

CHAPTER 2
❖ Ick-o-rama ❖

The woman set the bundle in Rose's arms. "Will you give this to the doll doctor?" she asked them.

Rose and Lila nodded again.

The woman smiled and gave her doll a gentle pat. Then she jogged away through the swirling, crackling fall leaves.

Rose and Lila shut the door. They weren't surprised that a doll had been delivered. Since their grandmother ran a doll hospital, people brought dolls to be fixed all the time. But most people weren't so mysterious about it.

"That lady was kind of weird," said Lila. "Why did she run off?"

"I don't know. Maybe she was late for a weirdo convention," said Rose. She ducked through the long strings of beads hanging in the living room doorway. Lila followed. The beads swayed and clacked as they went through.

Rose sat in a bowl-shaped orange swivel chair, with

the bundle on her lap. A note fell out, and she picked it up. On the outside, there was old-fashioned cursive writing.

Lila leaned over the back of the chair and poked her. "Open it."

Rose shook her head. "No. It says *To the Doll Doctor*." She set the note aside and unfolded the raggedy blankets so they could see the doll better.

Lila took one look and made a yucky face. "Ick-o-rama."

The cloth doll's flowery dress was frayed and stained. One of its burlap shoes was missing, and the other was coming apart. Its eyes, nose, and mouth were hand stitched with old, faded embroidery floss. The ragged green threads on one eye had come loose, so the doll looked like it was winking.

"And we thought Tatiana was a mess before she got fixed," said Rose.

"Who's a mess?" asked Far Nana. She came down the stairs two at a time. A tie-dyed scarf at the end of her long, gray braid fluttered out behind her. Her eyeglasses glittered. Tiny mirrors sewn onto her purple dress sparkled.

We probably have the only grandmother in town who's a hippie, thought Rose.

Five years ago, when Rose was five and Lila was

three, they'd nicknamed their grandmother "Far Nana." That was because she lived far away from their apartment back in the city. Far Nana was their mom's mother. They hadn't seen her very often before they came to live with her.

Near Nana was their dad's mother. The place where she lived was in the city, near their apartment, but it was only for older people. It didn't allow kids. So the girls couldn't live with her while their parents were in Africa.

Rose and Lila weren't sure Far Nana liked having them stay with her. She had lived alone for a long time and wasn't used to kids. They weren't sure they liked it, either. Everything was way different from home.

"Look, Far Nana! A lady brought you a doll," said Lila.

"And she left a note," said Rose.

"We didn't read it, though," said Lila. "Because it says *To the Doll Doctor*. And that's you."

Far Nana opened the note, holding it so Rose and Lila could see. Lila read aloud:

"*Dear Doll Doctor,*

I've looked for a good doll hospital for a long time.

Everyone says no one is better at fixing dolls than you are.

Please do what you can for my doll, Goldie.
I'll be back for her in a few days.
Thank you kindly,
Mrs. E. W. Shaw'

"I bet the E. W. stands for Extra Weird," Lila whispered to Rose.

Far Nana studied the doll in Rose's lap. "Not many people bring rag dolls in for repair."

"Can you fix it?" asked Rose.

"Maybe," said Far Nana.

"I wouldn't touch that doll with a ten-foot pole," said Lila.

"Or an eleven-foot one," said Rose. "It stinks." She put the doll down on the coffee table. Then she sniffed herself to be sure no doll stink had rubbed off.

CHAPTER 3
❧ Super-weird ❧

Far Nana looked at the girls and then at her watch. "I thought school started at eight-thirty. It's almost that time now."

"But Goldie just got here," said Lila. "Maybe we should stay home and help you fix her."

Far Nana nudged them toward the stairs. "My job is fixing dolls. Yours is going to school. You can help with Goldie later."

"Good try," Rose told Lila. They rushed upstairs to their bedroom and grabbed their backpacks.

Lila petted all four of Far Nana's cats on the way back down the stairs. "Bye, John. Bye, Paul and George. Bye, Ringo."

"C'mon, hurry up," said Rose. "I hate being late."

"Maybe you'd better start running on your crab legs, then," said Lila. "It's too bad we aren't back home in the city. Then you could take a taxi-crab to school."

"Ha-ha," said Rose. "And you could get there on your joke-mobile."

"Well, you could get there on your —" began Lila.

Rose screeched to a halt at the bottom of the stairs. "Oh, no," she whispered.

Lila almost fell over her. "What's wrong?"

Far Nana was standing by the front door, jangling her keys. She said the very words Rose dreaded hearing: "Thought I'd give you girls a ride to school."

Lila ran for the door. "Yay! I get the front."

Rose groaned. She didn't want anyone at her new school to think she and Lila were weird. And the weirdest thing about them was their grandmother. Her house was weird, her clothes were weird, and her cats were weird.

But worst of all was her super-weird van. It was rainbow-colored, with silly bumper stickers on the back. They said things like: HONK IF YOU LOVE DOLLS; MAKE DOLLS, NOT WAR; and HAVE YOU HUGGED A DOLL TODAY?

Rose did not want anyone to see them riding in that van.

But Far Nana rushed them out to the old van before Rose could think of an excuse.

"I hope nobody sees us," Rose whispered to Lila.

"I hope they do," said Lila.

Far Nana sat in the front seat beside Lila. Lila thumped the crystals hanging from the rearview mirror. They swung back and forth wildly as Far Nana drove away.

They lived just five blocks from their new school. But they must have driven past fifty kids on the way. Everyone else was walking.

"Look! There's Nadia!" said Lila.

Far Nana tooted her horn. It wasn't a normal one. It played a rock-and-roll song Rose had heard on the oldies radio station Far Nana listened to. The horn played on and on.

Lila and Far Nana waved. Nadia stared at them in surprise.

Rose slumped down, trying to hide. Nadia had seemed nice when they'd met her. And she had something else going for her. Unlike Far Nana, she had a TV and a computer.

Now Far Nana had probably blown Rose's chances of making friends with her. Great.

CHAPTER 4
❖ Dork Elementary ❖

The minute Far Nana stopped in front of the school, Rose leaped from the car. "Bye!" she yelled.

"Wait up!" shouted Lila.

Rose ducked her head and dashed in the front door of the school. She didn't stop until she got to the main hall. Lila caught up with her, huffing and puffing.

They stared at a big painting of a man that hung on the wall above them. A sign above the painting said WELCOME TO OAK HILL ELEMENTARY SCHOOL. Below the painting said OUR SCHOOL FOUNDER: MR. ARTHUR P. DORKOWITZ III.

"Here we are at Dork Elementary," said Rose.

Lila giggled like Rose had hoped she would. Then she darted a scared look at all the kids in the hallway around them. Some kids were talking about what they had done during summer vacation. Others were laughing or waving. They all seemed to be having fun.

Lila scooted closer to Rose. "Everybody has friends

except us. We don't know *anybody*. What if nobody likes us?"

Rose was worried about the same thing, but she didn't want Lila to know. Rose was the big sister. It was her job to be brave. "They will," she told Lila. "Just don't act weird. No spooky talk or counting people's tooth fillings or anything."

"Let's bump lockets for luck," said Lila. "That's what the Super-duper Dog Heroes on TV do. Only they bump dog tags. It makes them invisible."

"You mean invincible," said Rose, though right now she thought being invisible might be even better.

"What's the difference?" asked Lila.

"*Invisible* means no one can see you," said Rose. "*Invincible* means no one can beat you."

"I wish we could be both," said Lila.

Rose smiled. "Me, too."

The bell rang just as they tapped their lockets together.

"Ready?" asked Rose.

"Ready," said Lila.

Rose squeezed Lila's hand good-bye, and they headed in opposite directions.

Far Nana had taken Rose and Lila to visit the school a few days ago. It had felt funny being at school before it really opened. The teachers had been wearing T-shirts and shorts. They had been busy setting up their class-rooms. But Rose's and Lila's teachers had taken breaks to say hello.

Rose stopped in front of her classroom. The sign on the door said Ms. BEAN, FOURTH GRADE. She rubbed her golden locket for good luck and went inside.

Lots of other kids in Rose's class were wearing jeans like she was. She didn't look weird or different. So far, so good.

Ms. Bean was wearing a pink dress. She was short and plump, and she reminded Rose of a pink jelly bean. Ms. Bean had seemed okay a few days ago. But what if she had only been pretending to be nice in front of Far Nana?

"Ms. Bean, Ms. Bean. Hope you're not mean," Rose whispered to herself.

"Do you go to my school now?" someone beside Rose asked. It was next-door Nadia.

Rose nodded. "I didn't know it was yours, though. I thought it belonged to the guy hanging in the hall — Arthur P. Dorkowitz III."

Nadia grinned. "He gave it to me."

Rose grinned back. "Lucky you." She tried to think of something else to say. Something that would make Nadia like her. "I like your shoes," she said.

"Thanks. I like your necklace," said Nadia. "Does it have anything inside?"

15

Rose snapped her locket open and pointed at the pictures. "This is my mom, and that's my dad."

Nadia bent to take a closer look. "Are they dead?"

"No!" said Rose. She snapped the locket closed, almost catching Nadia's nose.

Nadia jumped back. "Hey!"

"My mom and dad are doctors," said Rose. "They're in Africa, helping sick people in small villages. But it's only for a year. When they come home, we're moving back to the city, where we belong."

"Okay! Don't get all mad," said Nadia. "Since you're living with your grandmother, I just wondered what happened to your parents."

"Sorry," said Rose. But she wasn't.

Rose found a good seat and slung her backpack over the chair.

"We don't do it like that here," said Nadia. "Backpacks go on those hooks by the cubbies."

"Marvelous," said Rose.

She hung her backpack on the only empty hook left. It slid off.

"That one's broken," said Nadia.

Rose sighed. "Stupendous."

"Wow. You know a lot of jawbreakers. You some kind of genius?" asked a boy. The name on his backpack said Bartholomew.

"No," said Rose. "What's a jawbreaker?"

"A word so big it almost cracks your jaw to say it," said the boy.

"Oh, like Bartholomew?" asked Rose.

He frowned at her. "It's Bart."

Rose hung her backpack sideways and wrapped its straps around the broken hook. It stayed.

Bart gave her a funny look. "You're weird."

"Fabulous," Rose grumbled to herself. "Just what I was hoping everyone would think."

That morning, Ms. Bean handed out schedules, school supply lists, and new books. They were starting American History, something Rose had already done in her old school. Easy, but boring.

How was she supposed to think about Thomas Jefferson on the very first day of school? There was too much else to worry about. Like did the other kids like her? Did she like them?

Rose wondered how Lila was doing in second grade. And how Far Nana was doing back home with Goldie.

CHAPTER 5
❖ Good and Bad ❖

Finally, it was lunchtime.

Red and yellow maple leaves blew onto the outdoor walkway that led to the cafeteria. They crunched under Rose's feet. Oak Hill Elementary had a grassy playground with trees and picnic tables. When it was warm enough, like today, everyone ate outside. It was nice.

Their old school hadn't even had a playground. Part of the street alongside the school had been blocked off so kids could play there during recess.

A real playground was better.

Rose made a list in her head called *Good and Bad Things About Moving Here.*

On the *Good Things* side:

Nice playground at school.

On the *Bad Things* side:

Can't find my stuff.

Don't have any friends.

Not sure Far Nana likes us.

Far Nana is weird.

Far Nana doesn't have a computer or TV.

Rose saw Lila playing kickball with some other kids. Lila shouldn't have worried. She never had any problem making friends.

But Rose had been hoping to hang around with Lila at lunch. Now what was she supposed to do?

Nadia walked by, holding a glittery blue lunch box. She looked at Rose's empty hands. "What are you having?"

Oh, no! Rose thought. She didn't have any lunch money! She stuck her hands in her jeans pockets. Her stomach rumbled. But she wasn't going to tell Nadia that her grandmother was so weird she'd forgotten about lunch money.

Before Rose could think of an answer, Lila ran over. "Far Nana forgot to give us lunch money!" she yelled.

Everybody heard.

Bart laughed. "Why would a banana give you lunch money?"

"Not banana," said Rose. "Far Nana."

"That's our grandmother," said Lila.

"Your grandmother is a banana?" Bart started scratching under his arms like a monkey. *"Ooh-ooh!"*

Nadia elbowed Bart away. "Sit with us," she told Rose and Lila. She pulled them to a nearby table where some other girls were eating.

Lila tugged on Rose's arm. "Let's call Far Nana. We need lunch money."

Rose shook her head no. She didn't want the other kids to find out Far Nana was a hippie. "Far Nana is probably too busy," she told Lila.

"So what are we going to do? Starve?" asked Lila.

Nadia opened a plastic container. "You want some of my mushroom soup?"

Rose and Lila looked at her like she was crazy. No way! Their nickname for mushroom soup was booger soup. Since Nadia was being so nice, they didn't tell her that, though.

A girl with short black hair slid them some chips on a napkin. "You can have these," she said.

Other kids pitched in, too. They gave Rose and Lila a box of juice, a milk, two unwanted half sandwiches, eleven candy corns, and an apple.

Lila handed the apple to Rose. "A crabby apple. Must be for you."

Rose didn't know what a real crab apple looked like. But she didn't feel so crabby anymore. So far, most of the kids at Oak Hill Elementary were nice.

She took a big bite. "I think maybe it's a not-so-crabby apple."

CHAPTER 6
❖ Checkup ❖

Far Nana looked surprised to see Rose and Lila when they got home after school. *Was she hoping we'd run away or something?* Rose wondered.

"I went garage-saling today. I got so busy, I didn't realize how much time had gone by," Far Nana told them.

"How do you sail a garage?" asked Lila.

"You've never been to a garage sale?" asked Far Nana.

"Nuh-uh." Lila shook her head.

"Well, we'll all have to go some weekend. They're fun. People sell things they don't want anymore," Far Nana explained. "You can find all sorts of bargains."

"Used stuff?" Rose wrinkled her nose.

Far Nana nodded. "But enough about my day. How was your first day of school?"

Rose shrugged. "Okay."

"School was cool!" said Lila. "I got to e-mail my friends back home."

"You did?" asked Rose.

"Yeah. My teacher, Mr. Yi, helped me in computer lab," said Lila. "Next time Mom and Dad call, I'm going to ask if I can e-mail them."

"I don't know if the little African village they're in will have e-mail. But it couldn't hurt to ask," said Far Nana.

"Everybody has e-mail!" said Lila. "If you bought a computer, you could e-mail them, too."

"If you're buying things, don't forget a TV. There's lots of educational stuff on TV," said Rose.

"Nice try. But TV is not my bag," said Far Nana.

"What?" asked Rose.

"Not my bag. That's what we said in the sixties to mean *who needs it*," explained Far Nana.

"*We* need it. We're dying of no-TV-itis." Rose grabbed her own neck and made a choking face.

"And no-e-mail-itis," said Lila. She pretend-choked herself, too.

Far Nana started twisting her bead necklaces, a sure sign she was getting nervous.

Rose decided to give her a break and change the subject. "How's Goldie?"

Far Nana smiled and stopped twisting her beads. "Let's get some snacks, and I'll show you."

In the kitchen, Lila got out the chocolate milk. Rose poured, filling two glasses as even-steven as she could. Then Lila got to choose which glass she wanted. That way, they always made extra-sure neither of them got more.

Far Nana was busy covering crackers with cheese and green stuff.

Lila poked the green stuff. "What are these weeds on top?"

"Sprouts, spinach, and dandelions," said Far Nana. "From my herb garden. Eat up. It's good for you."

"You first," Lila whispered to Rose.

Rose tried hers. "It's okay," she whispered back.

Lila took a bite and made a face. When Far Nana wasn't looking, she pulled the green stuff off her cracker and threw it away.

They all went upstairs to the witch's hat, munching. Four cats followed. Lila greeted each one by name.

"Ringo's easy to remember because he's black," Rose said. "But how can you tell the three gray ones apart?"

"They're all a little different," said Lila. "John has green eyes, and Paul has a gray nose."

"What about George?" asked Rose.

Lila picked George up. She held up one of his paws so Rose could see the bottom. "Pink toes."

Far Nana opened the door to the witch's hat. Inside, her doll hospital stuff filled the whole room. Buttons, yarn, fabric, ribbons, and scissors sat on shelves and hung out of drawers. There were boxes and bags of doll parts like eyeballs, shoes, and wigs. There were lots of dolls, too: big dolls, little dolls, and in-between-size dolls.

A rag doll was sitting by the window. It was Goldie, but her dress and shoes were gone!

"What did you do to Goldie?" asked Rose.

"I thought you were going to wait for us," said Lila.

"I've been giving her a checkup," said Far Nana. "I'm afraid the news is pretty bad. Goldie needs a lot of work."

"Why does that lady want you to fix a junky rag doll like this, anyway?" asked Rose. "Why doesn't she just throw it away and buy a new doll?"

"It's true that it will cost more to fix her than it would to buy a new doll," said Far Nana. "I imagine Goldie must be very special to Mrs. Shaw."

"Goldie doesn't look special," said Lila. She put one hand over her mouth and leaned over to Far Nana. "Goldie can't hear us, can she? I don't want to hurt her feelings. She can't help it if she's stinky."

When they had helped fix Nadia's doll a few weeks ago, Rose and Lila had learned something amazing. Far Nana could talk to dolls! At least, Rose and Lila thought she could. They weren't really sure they believed it yet.

"I'm sure Goldie understands," said Far Nana. "She knows she has seen better days."

"How did she get like this?" asked Rose. "Did she tell you?"

"I've been saving her story until you got home. It starts way back in 1929," said Far Nana. "But it's her story, so I'll let her tell it."

Far Nana wrapped Goldie in the cloth bundle she had come in and propped her on a pillow. The afternoon sun shone on the rag doll, highlighting every stain and frayed thread.

Far Nana stared into Goldie's eyes. Nothing happened for a few seconds.

Then Far Nana began to speak softly. And Goldie began her story. . . .

CHAPTER 7
❖ Goldie's Story ❖
A One-of-a-Kind Doll

I wasn't always a rag doll.

I started out as a factory-made doll. I was made of plastic-like stuff called composition that was pressed into a doll mold. When I popped out of my mold, I was given gray eyes that opened and shut. Then I was painted and given a blond wig and a dress.

I was a Happy Abby doll. But I wasn't happy.

I looked just like hundreds of other shiny-faced Happy Abby dolls. All of us wore ruffled dresses and had mohair wigs curled into ringlets. Some of us had hair or dresses of different colors. Other than that, we were all exactly the same.

The other Happy Abbys didn't seem to mind being look-alikes. But I dreamed of being a one-of-a-kind doll. I wanted to be special.

Whenever orders came in, dolls were put into boxes and sent out through the big factory doors. It was scary, not knowing when my turn would come. Or where I

27

would go. None of us knew where dolls went when they left the factory.

Oh, there was gossip.

I heard that dolls go live with kind children who love them, said a Happy Abby on the shelf above me.

I heard that dolls get to play with their children, said another Happy Abby.

The grim doll next to me shook her head. She had been bought from the factory a month ago but had been returned. *Not all children are kind and loving,* she told us. *My girl dragged me around by my hair. I was sent back here to be fixed because she poked out my eye!*

We all gasped. The grim Happy Abby was wise and had seen the world. We had to believe her. But surely not all children were so awful.

I wished for a girl who would love me.

One September day, a man in a suit came into the factory. He showed a picture of a little girl to one of the workers. I could see it from where I sat. The girl had green eyes. Her short blond hair was tied with a green bow. She wore a knee-length green silk dress, white stockings, and black shoes with buckles.

"A rich banker and his wife special-ordered a Happy Abby from our catalog," the man in the suit said. "They want her dressed like their daughter in this picture. Pronto."

The worker took the photo, grabbed me from my shelf, and headed toward the factory.

My turn had come! It happened so fast I barely had time to say good-bye to my friends.

The other Happy Abbys gave me a cheery send-off. *Good luck,* they called after me.

You'll need it, muttered the grim Happy Abby.

I tried not to listen to her.

Back in the factory, my hair and clothes were quickly changed. My golden hair was cut short and tied with a green bow just like the little girl's in the photo. The seamstresses made me a swell green dress like hers, too. I even got new green eyes to replace my gray ones.

When I was finished, I looked different from all the other Happy Abbys. In many ways, I was still just like them. But I was glad to be even a little special.

I was put into a box and shipped by airmail.

I couldn't wait to meet my girl.

CHAPTER 8
✦ Goldie's Story ✦
My Girl

I arrived at a house and was taken straight from my box to sit on my girl's lap. I loved her on sight.

She looked down at me, smiled, and patted my golden hair. "Hey! You have goldie locks. Your name must be Goldie!"

"Silence, Eliza!" a man warned.

So my girl's name was Eliza. And she had given me a new name! Goldie. I liked it.

I waited for her to begin playing with me. But she just sat stiffly, with one arm curled around me. Two older girls sat on chairs beside her. They looked just alike — twins! Both girls had light brown hair curled in ringlets. One wore a red hair bow, and the other wore a violet hair bow. Each twin was holding a doll dressed to match her.

Were children always so still? What was going on?

The grumpy man who had scolded Eliza stared at

the girls. Then he dipped a paintbrush into some paint and brushed it on a big square canvas.

Now I got it. The girls were posing for a portrait!

The man painted all afternoon.

My girl never spoke to me. She didn't dare. If she or the other girls even scratched their noses, the painter would say, "Be still!"

Finally he put down his brushes. "You may go," he told them.

Hooray! Now playtime would begin, I thought.

But Eliza just tossed me on her chair and ran off after the twins.

The other two dolls were left on the chairs beside me.

I'm Ruby, the doll with a red dress and a matching red hair bow told me.

I'm Violet, said the doll wearing a violet-flowered dress and a violet bow.

I'm Happy Ab — I mean, I'm Goldie, I told them. *Eliza is my girl.*

Eliza's sisters belong to us, said Ruby.

Aha! So the twins were Eliza's sisters.

Why don't our girls play with us? I asked.

The artist doesn't want us to get dirty. They can't play with us until the painting is finished, said Ruby.

We're our girls' favorite dolls, said Violet. *That's why we're being included in the painting.*

Am I Eliza's favorite? I asked.

Violet giggled. *Eliza doesn't have a favorite. She thinks dolls are sissy.*

Eliza is a tomboy, said Ruby.

My new girl was a tomboy?

I was doomed.

CHAPTER 9
❖ Goldie's Story ❖
Stuck-up

*T*he artist returned to paint the next afternoon. Again, we sat still for hours. Afterward the girls left us on the chairs as they had the day before. The same thing happened the next day and the next.

One afternoon, the painter swished a last dab of paint onto the canvas. Then he laid down his brushes. *"Fini!"*

That's French, whispered Ruby. *He means the painting is finished.*

Eliza leaped from her chair. She grabbed me by one arm and dashed down the hall. I didn't even have time to say good-bye to Ruby and Violet.

I bounced along, dangling from Eliza's fingers. She ran into her room and slammed the door behind us.

Now we will play, I thought.

"I'm glad that's finished," said Eliza. "Up you go, Goldie." She tossed me onto a shelf.

She yanked off her dress and pulled on a shirt and overalls. Then she opened the window and grabbed a

tree branch. Lickety-split, she slid down the tree and out of sight.

I was disappointed. But there would be other chances to make friends with my girl.

Eliza's bedroom was messy. Tin soldiers, a train, balls, tangled jump ropes, and other toys covered the floor.

Worst of all, there were nine other dolls! Eliza would never notice me with so many more beautiful dolls to choose from.

Excuse me, I said to the dolls. *When does Eliza play with us?*

She's not allowed to play with us, said a lovely china doll wearing a pink velvet dress and gloves. *We're too expensive.*

And be thankful for that, said a nearby doll. She was made of bisque and wore a pleated gray silk dress and cape. *Eliza broke the last doll she played with in a game of cowboys and Indians.*

So the doll at the factory was right, I said. *Children do hurt dolls.*

Hmmph! You're a factory-made doll? The china doll twitched her velvet skirt away from me like I smelled bad.

When did the family start letting in such riffraff! What's the world coming to? said the bisque doll.

What kind of name is Goldie, anyway? asked the

porcelain doll by the window. She wore a beautiful ivory-colored lace dress and matching earrings.

Eliza named me that because my hair is golden, I said.

You're nothing special, said the china doll. *Eliza will forget you like the rest of us.*

She turned out to be right. For weeks, Eliza didn't pick me up. I sat still and alone, gathering dust.

Her stuck-up dolls ignored me, but they talked among themselves. I listened and learned what I could.

The porcelain doll was closest to the window, so she was our lookout. She told us what was going on in the world outside. At least, what she could see of it.

She often said things like, *Eliza's mother is leaving. She's wearing her favorite yellow shawl and a new dress and hat. She must be going to a tea party today. Or perhaps to a garden club meeting.*

We didn't see much of the twins. They were older than Eliza and ignored her most of the time. Eliza's mother or father brought her a new toy every now and then. A tutor and someone named Nanny came every day. But Eliza didn't seem to have any friends.

No one except me noticed she was lonely.

I was, too.

CHAPTER 10
❖ Goldie's Story ❖
Trouble

One October night, the porcelain lookout doll announced, *Eliza's father is home from his job at the bank.*

Late again, said the china doll.

That's six nights in a row, said the bisque doll.

He looks worried, reported the porcelain doll.

Minutes later, we heard Eliza's father talking to her mother as they passed in the hallway. "Black Tuesday . . . stock market crash . . ." He sounded upset.

"Depression." We heard Eliza's parents say the word over and over during the next few weeks. What did it mean?

It meant trouble, I soon found out.

Eliza's mother didn't go out much anymore. And her father stopped going to the bank.

One day, the tutor and Nanny didn't come. Eliza's mother came to our room instead. She was carrying an empty suitcase.

Eliza stopped the project she was working on and jumped up. "Mother, look! I'm making a scootermobile. It's going to have spinners and . . . What are you doing?"

Her mother had begun packing Eliza's clothes into the suitcase. "Come here, dear." She patted the bed, and Eliza went to sit next to her. "I have some troubling news. The reason your tutor and Nanny didn't come today is that we had to let them go. We simply couldn't pay them anymore."

Eliza looked surprised. "Nanny and the tutor got paid? How much?"

"That's not important now. There's more. Your father and I waited as long as we could to tell you this, so you wouldn't worry. But now . . . now, it's time." Her mother took a deep breath. "Because of the Depression, many businesses have failed recently. A few weeks ago, the bank where your father worked failed, too. The owner stole what money was left in the bank and skipped town."

The other dolls and I gasped.

"Oh, no!" said Eliza.

"Unfortunately, many people are angry at your father."

"It wasn't his fault!"

Her mother sighed. "That doesn't matter. Your father and the owner were partners, so it's up to us to pay back the stolen money. That means we're going to have to sell our house. We'll have to move."

"Move? Where?" asked Eliza. She sounded scared.

"My brother, your Uncle Ned, has a little cabin we can live in."

"A cabin? Like Daniel Boone?"

"Sort of. Only this one's on your uncle's farm. The farm I grew up on."

"Is it a log cabin? Can I wear a raccoon-tail hat?" Eliza asked.

She sounded excited. Maybe our new home would be fun.

"We'll see. Things are going to be hard for a while. We won't have much money or room where we're going. Almost everything in the house will have to be sold to help pay back the bank. I'm afraid that includes your toys."

The other dolls groaned. This was a disaster!

Eliza tried to be brave. "I don't need toys. Daniel Boone didn't have toys, either, I bet."

Her mother smiled. "I'm glad you're looking on the bright side." She finished packing Eliza's suitcase and turned to go. "You and your sisters can each keep your favorite doll, but that's all. Choose one, and hang on to it, so the moving trucks don't take it tomorrow."

I held my breath at this news. Which of us would Eliza choose? I knew I wasn't special enough for her to pick me. But still, I hoped.

Eliza shrugged. "I don't like dolls. Can't I take my scootermobile instead?"

Her mother shook her head. "No, there won't be enough room in the car."

"Daniel Boone didn't have dolls." Eliza crossed her arms and pouted.

"No. But the children in his fort probably did," said her mother.

"And I bet he protected them from bad guys," said Eliza.

"I bet he did." Her mother smiled and gave Eliza a hug.

After her mother left with the suitcase, Eliza got busy. She set two chairs at the foot of her bed and draped a blanket over the chair backs and the two bedposts. It made a sort of tent. What was she doing?

Eliza hurried over to our shelf. She reached for the beautiful china doll. Then she noticed me.

"Hey, Goldie! I remember you. You're the one who looks like me."

She grabbed me instead of the china doll and ran back to the tent she'd built. We got inside.

Eliza peeked out from underneath the blanket.

Pow! Pow! She pretended to shoot imaginary bad guys.

She held me up and pretended to make me talk. "Help! Help!" she cried in a squeaky voice.

"Never fear," she answered in a lower voice. "I'll save you. I will protect our cabin, for I am Daniel Boone."

I didn't really pay attention to what she was saying. I was still in shock because —

Eliza had chosen me.

CHAPTER 11
❧ Goldie's Story ❧
Everything Goes

*T*he next morning, a rumbling sound woke me. I was warm, snuggled in Eliza's bed beside her. I had never slept lying down before. It was so comfortable, I didn't want to move.

Big trucks, warned the porcelain lookout doll on the nearby shelf. *Five of them.*

The trucks woke Eliza, too. She got dressed and carried me over to her second-story window. In the front driveway below us, men in coveralls were swarming around big trucks like bees.

There was writing on the sides of the trucks. "Mo's Moving Company," read Eliza. "Uh-oh. This is scarier than I thought it would be. I don't want to leave. And I don't want those movers coming in here."

The men came into the house. We heard their voices downstairs.

A few minutes later, the knob on Eliza's door began

to turn. She slipped silently into her tent, taking me with her.

The door opened, and two of the moving men came in. Eliza and I spied on them from our tent, but they didn't see us. One of the men waved his arm wide toward Eliza's things. "Everything goes," he told the other man, who was holding a clipboard. The clipboard man wrote something down, and they went back out.

Eliza ran over to her door and slammed it hard behind them. She pushed her toy box across the room until it blocked the door.

Then she joined me in the tent again. "That'll keep them out."

We heard the men talking as they went in and out of other rooms down the hall.

More moving men were at Eliza's door within minutes. They tried to open it. When they couldn't get in, they knocked loudly. "Hey! Open up."

Eliza wrapped both arms around me. "Don't worry, Goldie. I'll save you, for I am Daniel Boone."

The men shoved, and the toy box began to move. The door opened slowly. They were in!

Two men began putting Eliza's toys into boxes. Another man walked over to our tent and yanked the blanket off. He stared at us in surprise.

Eliza jumped up, dropping me. "Get lost!" she shouted.

"Sorry, little lady. We've got orders to pack this stuff and take it away." He took the chairs and blanket, and our tent disappeared.

"I'm getting out of here before you pack me, too!" Eliza ran to the window and grabbed the tree branch. She swung one leg over the sill. She was leaving!

Wait! You forgot me! I shouted.

Eliza froze. Had she heard me? She hopped back inside and stared at me.

Take me with you! I begged.

"You can't have everything," she told the man. "Mother said I get to keep my favorite doll."

The man shrugged. "Go ahead."

Eliza ran over, grabbed me, and rushed back to the window. She tucked me in the back of her overalls and climbed down the tree.

"I know the perfect hideout," she told me when we reached the ground. "Those men won't get us." She looked back at the house to be sure no one was watching. Then she ran under the droopy branches of a willow tree along the driveway.

She pulled me out and set me on her lap. "We can spy on the trucks from here," she said.

All day, we watched the men take tables, chairs, rugs,

and big boxes from the house. Even the painting of Eliza and her sisters was packed. The trucks rumbled past, going to and from the house, taking everything away to be sold.

After the last truck was gone, we crept back inside the house.

CHAPTER 12
❖ Goldie's Story ❖
Empty

Eliza's footsteps echoed on the stairs as we went up to her room. The house was empty.

So was Eliza's room, except for one thing. On the shelf where I'd once sat lay a tiny pink velvet glove. It was the china doll's! It looked lonely. I knew the china doll would miss it.

"There you are!" Eliza's mother came in. "I've been looking for you." She hurried us downstairs and into the car waiting in the garage.

The twins were already in the rumble seat, crying. I was glad to see Ruby and Violet were with them.

Isn't this awful? Ruby asked me.

Terrible, added Violet.

Yes, I agreed. *At least we aren't packed inside one of those trucks.*

Eliza cuddled me in her arms as we drove away. All of the family's remaining things were crammed into their car with us.

Before today, I had seen only the inside of the factory and Eliza's house. Now as the miles passed, I saw many other grand homes.

The landscape changed, and I saw bridges and tall buildings. Those gave way to farm fields with hay bales, barns, and cows.

It was dark and the twins were asleep when we finally stopped in front of a white farmhouse. It had black shutters and a wide porch with a swing. There was a barn nearby and shadowy plowed fields beyond it.

Eliza leaned forward. "This isn't a cabin!" she said. "This is Uncle Ned's house."

"Hush, Eliza," her mother said from the front seat. Eliza sat back, frowning.

Her mother and father went into the house and came back out with a man. The moonlight glinted off his curly red hair.

"Hi, Uncle Ned!" shouted Eliza.

Eliza's uncle smiled and waved. The grown-ups stood on the porch and talked for a few minutes. Her uncle went back inside, and we drove off again.

Eliza's shouting had woken the twins. "Where are we going?" one of them asked.

The other twin rubbed her eyes and yawned. "I have to go to the bathroom."

"We'll be there in a minute," said their mother.

Seconds later, we stopped in front of a small gray wooden shack.

"This is it," said their mother.

"I don't want to live here!" said one twin.

"Me, either," said the other.

"Quiet!" boomed their father. The girls fell silent.

Eliza and her sisters followed their parents inside the shack. Ruby and Violet got left behind in the car. Eliza took me with her.

Their mother showed us a room at the end of a short hall. It had three small beds. "This is where you girls will sleep."

"You mean we have to share a room?" asked one of the twins.

"With Eliza?" added the other one.

Their mother nodded. "Your father and I will sleep in the living room on a bed your uncle loaned us."

The girls' father brought their suitcases in and set them on the floor.

Eliza rubbed her hand across the wall. "Why is newspaper stuck all over the walls in here?"

"It keeps wind from blowing in through the boards on the outside of the house," said her father. He sounded embarrassed, as if he didn't like Eliza noticing such things.

"But where is the wallpaper? I want the kind with cowboys, like I had in my bedroom at home," said Eliza.

"We can't afford that anymore," said her mother.

Eliza's father looked sad. "I'm sorry it has come to this. I hate to think of my family living in a shack."

"It's clean and safe. And it's not forever," said Eliza's mother. She patted his arm. "Be thankful we aren't homeless. After all, beggars can't be choosers."

"Beggars?" Eliza whispered to me. "Is that what we are now?"

CHAPTER 13
⋇ Poor Nana? ⋇

Grrr! Rose's stomach growled.

"Must be time for supper," said Far Nana.

Rose and Lila blinked. Coming back to the present felt like waking up from a dream. It took a while to get used to it.

"Let's go eat," said Far Nana. "It's getting late. You girls must be starving."

Far Nana was right. While they'd been listening to Goldie's story, the sun had begun to set. It was getting dark in the witch's hat. And they *were* starving. But they wanted to keep listening to Goldie.

"I'm not hungry yet," said Rose.

"Me, either," said Lila. "Let's hear more of Goldie's story. I want to find out how she changed from a factory-made doll into a raggedy cloth one."

"Another day. Goldie needs rest, and we have things to do," said Far Nana. She headed down to the kitchen, so Rose and Lila did, too.

Far Nana's cooking was just as weird as everything

else about her. That night, she made spinach crepes with fruit faces. They had orange-slice mouths, strawberry eyes, and banana-slice noses.

But this time Lila didn't pick anything off. The crepes tasted great!

After supper, Rose and Lila cleared off the table and did their homework. Then Far Nana got out a bunch of letters and her checkbook.

"I've got a ton of bills to pay," she told Rose and Lila. "You girls go enjoy yourselves."

"Doing what?" asked Rose.

"There's nothing to do," said Lila.

"What did you do for fun back home?" asked Far Nana.

"Watch TV," said Rose.

"Play on the computer," said Lila.

Far Nana rolled her eyes. "I had to ask. Well, why don't you do what kids did during the Great Depression? They made up their own games. Or they played board games. I've got some of those in the living room closet. Go take a look."

Rose and Lila checked out the closet. Far Nana had old board games they'd never heard of. Lila read some of the names: "Rock and Troll; Beatnik Bingo; The Groovy Movie Game."

None of them looked like fun.

"I think she meant b-o-r-e-d games," said Rose.

"They're better than nothing," said Lila. With her eyes closed, she reached in and picked one.

It was called Dream Date. There were hearts and pictures of goofy guys on the front of the box.

Rose grinned. "This game is gonna be bizarro. I can already tell."

Lila spun the Dream Date spinner first. It landed on a nerdy guy. His hair stuck out in all directions. He was wearing a polka-dotted bow tie and purple plaid suspenders.

"Your future husband," teased Rose.

Lila made a face at her.

Next, Rose spun. Her guy was even worse. He had a piggy-looking nose and wore a rainbow-colored beanie with a red propeller on top.

"Trade you," said Rose.

"You wish," said Lila.

The game was so much fun that they played until bedtime. The cats joined in, chasing the spinner and pouncing on the cards.

They could hear Far Nana in the kitchen, clucking over the bills every now and then.

Later that night, Rose and Lila lay in their bunk beds in their mother's old bedroom. Rose heard Lila open her locket. She opened hers, too. They both kissed their mom's and dad's pictures as they did every night.

www.scholastic.com/titles/dollhospital

ISBN: B-KM9-40179-8

Doll Hospital   Goldie

SCHOLASTIC   Copyright © 2002 by Scholastic Inc.

Take a closer look at Goldie's world, find beautiful clothes
for her, and learn more about Doll Hospital at
www.scholastic.com/titles/dollhospital

Click! Click! Their lockets shut, sealing their parents away again.

"We have to remember to ask Far Nana for lunch money tomorrow," Lila said. "We can't keep mooching off the other kids."

"I don't want to ask her," said Rose. "I think she's poor."

Lila snapped on her lamp and looked down at Rose from the top bunk. "Why do you think that?"

"She shops at garage sales." Rose counted off on her fingers. "She eats weeds from her yard for snacks. Her van is twice as old as me. Her hippie clothes are *waaay* out of style. And did you see that pile of bills?"

"What about school supplies?" asked Lila. "We can make lunches. But notebooks cost money. You have to buy them."

"We'll ask Mom and Dad for money when they call tomorrow night," said Rose.

"But what about lunch and stuff for school tomorrow?" asked Lila.

Rose sighed. "Too bad Far Nana doesn't have a Monopoly game. At least then we'd have lunch money, even if it was fake."

CHAPTER 14
❖ All Wet ❖

The next morning, Rose set two paper sacks on the kitchen counter. She dropped a peanut butter and jelly sandwich and a bag of chips in each.

"Two slime and rockwiches plus chips," counted Lila. "What else is there?"

Rose got a box of granola bars out of the cupboard and looked inside it. "There's only one bar left," she said, pulling it out.

Lila leaned over and licked its wrapper. "Mine."

Rose shoved her. "Eew!"

Lila laughed and wiggled her eyebrows. She grabbed the granola bar and stuffed it into her sack.

Rose stuck a juice box into her own sack. "If you get the last granola bar, then I get the last juice."

"Why is there only one of everything? Are we running out of food?" asked Lila. "Maybe we're poor like Goldie and Eliza."

"Far Nana probably just forgot to buy groceries," said Rose. But she wasn't sure.

Rose ran up to the witch's hat to tell Far Nana good-bye before they left for school. She heard splashing noises. Far Nana was washing something in a small tub. Rose went closer.

It was Goldie! She was wet. And flat.

"What happened to Goldie?" Rose asked.

"As you girls noted, she was a little musty and stained. I unstuffed her so I could wash her," said Far Nana.

Rose knew Far Nana could put Goldie back together again. Still, it was strange to see Goldie like this. "I won't ever get used to this part of fixing dolls. The part where they look worse before they look better," Rose said.

"Goldie will feel a lot better once she's clean," said Far Nana.

"What happens then?" asked Rose.

Far Nana held Goldie's flat, dripping-wet body up to the light so Rose could see. "The cloth has worn so thin, you can almost see through her. I'm afraid she'll rip soon. So after she dries, I'm going to line her body with lightweight material. That will make it stronger. And that way, we save as much of the old doll as possible."

"I wish I could help you today instead of going to school," said Rose.

Far Nana didn't say, "I wish you could, too" or anything like that. She just put Goldie back in the tub and kept washing.

Lila called from downstairs. "C'mon, Rose. Hurry up!"

"Would you girls like a ride again?" Far Nana asked.

Rose stepped back. "No way! I mean, uh, we have enough time to walk to school. See you!" She dashed down the stairs and out the front door.

CHAPTER 15
❖ The Dream Team ❖

Don't be afraid to get wet in the sea of knowledge," Ms. Bean told the class.

Rose and the rest of the kids opened their books for silent reading.

The desks in Ms. Bean's room were grouped in teams of four. Rose's team had Nadia and a girl with short black hair named Emma. And Bart.

Rose looked up at the signs Ms. Bean had hung on strings above each team's desks. One of them said:

SOLVING: WE EACH TRY TO SOLVE OUR OWN PROBLEMS.

How was she supposed to do that? She couldn't snap her fingers and make money out of thin air. Or paper. And she needed some of that to write her report on the book she had picked out, *Mystery Mansion*.

She read another sign.

QUESTIONS: ASK YOUR TEAMMATES FOR HELP BEFORE ASKING THE TEACHER.

Rose looked at her team members. Nadia was reading about lost treasure. Emma was reading about soccer. Bart wasn't reading. He was hiding behind a book about magic. He didn't want Ms. Bean to see him playing a small handheld computer game called Wizard Battle.

"Can I borrow some paper?" Rose whispered to Nadia. "I forgot my notebook."

"Sure," said Nadia. She slid two sheets toward Rose.

Bart's head popped up from behind his book. "You forget your notebook every day. Why don't you write a note to yourself to remember your notepaper?" He laughed.

Rose wanted to tell him to mind his own business. But the sign above her said:

Courtesy: Show appreciation and be polite.

"Thanks. Good idea," Rose told him. She went back to reading. Bart went back to battling wizards.

On the first day, they had all chosen names for their teams. Some of the other team names were the Pumas, the Red Dragons, and the Diamond Snakes. Rose's group was the Dream Team. Her team wasn't exactly a dream with Bart around, though.

More like a nightmare.

CHAPTER 16
❖ The Face Snatchers ❖

By the time Rose and Lila got home from school, Goldie was dry.

The girls dropped their backpacks on the floor of the witch's hat. Rose leaned on one side of Far Nana to see what she was doing. Lila leaned on the other.

The pile of Goldie's old stuffing was all gone. So was something else.

Rose gasped. "Her face is missing!"

"Oooh!" Lila said in a spooky voice. "The face snatchers strike again!"

"Goldie's eyes, nose, and mouth threads were just too frayed to keep. I had to pull them out." Far Nana pointed to the bulletin board on the wall where pictures of Goldie were tacked. "I took instant photos before I did it. They'll help me make a new face that looks the same."

"I guess this means Goldie can't talk tonight," said Lila.

"Duh. Obviously. She doesn't even have a mouth," said Rose.

Far Nana laughed. "Don't worry. I'm going to restitch her face now."

"Can we watch?" asked Lila. "Just until Mom and Dad call. They said they'd call tonight."

"We could do our homework. We won't get in the way." Rose got out her books before Far Nana could say no.

"Okay," said Far Nana. "I've got a lot to do, though."

Lila got out her books, too. "I won't bother you." She was quiet for about two seconds.

When Far Nana got out some faded-looking embroidery floss, Lila leaned closer to see it. "Are you going to sew Goldie a new face with that?"

Rose nudged Lila. "Don't bother Far Nana while she's working."

"I'm not, am I?" Lila looked at Far Nana.

"It's nice that you're interested, and I'll gladly show you what I'm doing. After that, I'll need quiet so I can work," said Far Nana.

"Okay," said Lila.

Far Nana showed them the floss. "I dyed this to match the threads I removed from her face. I've got green for her eyes and gray-black for her eyebrows and eyelashes. And here's a nice soft pink for her lips and beige for her nose."

"Why did you have to dye it?" asked Rose.

"Because the bright colors of new floss would look out of place on an old doll like Goldie. I make it look older by dyeing or bleaching it."

Far Nana picked up a used, crinkled envelope with words handwritten on the back. It was a list of work she needed to do on Goldie. There were check marks by things she had already done.

Lila elbowed Rose and whispered, "She makes lists on old envelopes. Maybe she can't even afford to buy paper!"

"Told you," Rose whispered back.

Far Nana held up an old burlap sack. "Tomorrow, I'll reweave Goldie's burlap shoe using some threads from this potato sack. Then I'll use part of the sack to make a matching shoe for her other foot. That will just about do it. Except for one thing. I still need to find some yarn to match her hair."

"Oh, no!" said Lila. "Do you have to throw her golden hair away? That's what makes Goldie Goldie."

Far Nana flipped Goldie's yarn hair up. There were bald places where some of it had fallen out. "I'm going to keep her hair. But I need more to fill in for the pieces that have been lost. Matching yarn is not going to be easy to find. I'll have to dye some. And I'll have to rough it up so it looks older than it really is."

Looking at Goldie's hair gave Rose an idea. She ran

to her room, got something from her drawer, and ran back. She showed Far Nana the triangle-shaped knitted yellow hair scarf she'd gotten. "How about this? We could pull it apart and use some of these yarn threads. They're yellow and kind of old like Goldie's hair."

Far Nana lay the stretchy scarf against Goldie's hair. "Amazing. It's a perfect match! But are you certain you want to give this up?"

"Well —" Rose began uncertainly.

"You have to help Goldie!" Lila butted in.

Rose wasn't sure what to do. The scarf was her favorite because her mom had made it. She wanted to keep it. But she wanted to help Goldie, too.

"I think I can take all the yarn I need from the edges of your scarf," said Far Nana. "That way, your scarf will become a bit smaller. But you can still wear it."

"Okay," said Rose. "Good idea. Goldie needs the yarn more than my scarf does."

Far Nana smiled. "I'm sure Goldie appreciates it. Now it's work time." She sat down and began sewing a new face for Goldie.

It was hard to do homework when something so exciting was going on. Rose and Lila peeked every now and then. Far Nana didn't seem to mind too much. At least she didn't yell or anything. It was fun watching her fix Goldie.

Still, Rose and Lila were a little worried.

"I wonder why Mom and Dad haven't called yet," said Rose.

"They're probably just busy. They'll call," said Far Nana.

But they didn't.

CHAPTER 17
❖ Feeling Better ❖

Mr. Yi only has two tooth fillings," Lila told Rose on the way home from school the next day.

Rose didn't say anything.

"Far Nana has six," Lila added.

"Are you writing a book or something?" asked Rose. "Who cares?"

"Yes, I am writing a book, for your information. Mr. Yi said we have to fill a notebook by next summer. We each have to think of a topic. I'm going to make a list of everyone I meet this whole year. And I'll write how many tooth fillings they have. And how many freckles. Spy stuff like that. But first, I need a notebook."

"Yeah, and Ms. Bean gave us a list of supplies to buy," said Rose. "Since Mom and Dad didn't call, somebody has to ask Far Nana for money."

"You," Rose and Lila said at almost the same time. Lila had said it a little sooner. "I win," she said.

"If I ask her, then you have to ask her the next hard thing," said Rose.

"Deal," said Lila.

Lila rushed up the stairs to the witch's hat. Rose followed slowly.

"Did Mom and Dad call?" Rose heard Lila ask.

"Not yet. They will, though," Far Nana answered. "I'm sure of it."

Then Rose heard Lila say, "Wow! Goldie looks way better!"

Rose hurried the rest of the way up. "Wow is right," she said when she saw Goldie.

Goldie's new face looked the same as before, only nicer. She was stuffed again. And her golden hair was thick and pretty.

Rose and Lila sniffed the doll and smiled. "No stink!" they said at the same time.

Far Nana wrapped Goldie in her blanket and set her on a pillow. "Now that Goldie's feeling better, I think she's ready to go on with her story. But your homework comes first."

"No homework today," said Lila.

"Me, either," said Rose. "I did it at lunch."

"Okay, then," said Far Nana. "I'll mend Goldie's dress while we listen."

Rose was glad she could put off asking about money.

She and Lila got comfortable, Rose in the wicker chair and Lila on the rug. The cats snuggled in with them.

Far Nana stared at Goldie like she could see what was going on inside her. After a few seconds, Far Nana began to speak. And Goldie's story continued.

CHAPTER 18
⁘ Goldie's Story ⁘
A Hard Life

*E*liza pulled me close. "This isn't a Daniel Boone cabin. I think it's the poorhouse," she told me.

In the morning sunlight, our new home did look bad. The wood floor was so old and dry it had splinters. The braided rug in the living room was worn flat as cardboard. Window curtains that had once been blue were now faded gray.

"I'm hungry," one of the twins said.

Eliza's mother got out some food: bread, cheese, and milk. It wasn't much.

"Is this all we have?" asked the other twin.

"We didn't have room for more in the car," said their mother. "I'll go up to the farmhouse for food later." She looked around the shack and sighed. "I left this farm for the city years ago. I never wanted to come back. It's a hard life."

"Are we going to starve?" Eliza asked in a small voice.

"Oh, honey, no!" Her mother gave Eliza a quick squeeze. "We'll plant a garden out back. And we have chickens to lay eggs. We won't starve."

"But we need money, right?" said Eliza.

"I'll take in sewing, and your father will help your uncle on the farm. We'll get by," said their mother. "I'll need your help, too. Let's go to the chicken coop, and I'll show you how to gather eggs."

Her mother tugged on me, trying to pull me out of Eliza's hands. "Leave Goldie inside. She'll get dirty."

Eliza held on to me tight. "No! I need her!"

Her mother let go. "All right. Just be careful."

Out at the chicken coop, Eliza made sure not to smudge my clothes. A bit of dirt got on my cheek, and she wiped it off gently. After a while, she tucked me inside the front bib of her overalls so she could pick up eggs with both hands. I didn't mind. I could still see what was going on.

From then on, Eliza took me everywhere.

Except school. I wasn't allowed to go there with her. But she told me what happened the minute she got home.

"The schoolhouse has four rooms, with two grades in each room," she told me. "There aren't enough desks for everyone, so we share. The teacher is kind of grumpy. If you do something wrong, he smacks your hands with a wooden ruler! I liked my old tutor better.

"And guess what? The other kids are even poorer than we are. There's one boy whose pants are so old they have about a million holes. The other kids call him Holey Joe. It's not funny, really. It's sad."

One night, Eliza and I heard her mother crying. It wasn't the first time.

Eliza snuggled closer. "When grown-ups cry, you know there's really something wrong," she whispered. "If I had some money, I would buy our old house back. Then Mother wouldn't cry. I wish I had something I could sell."

Suddenly, Eliza pulled away and stared at me! No! Surely, she wouldn't. She couldn't. Was she planning to sell *me*?

"Don't worry, Goldie. It'll be okay," Eliza told me. I think she was trying to make herself believe it.

CHAPTER 19
❧ Goldie's Story ❧
The Pawnshop

*T*o my surprise, Eliza took me with her when she left for school the next morning. She hid me inside her coat before leaving the shack with the twins. I was excited about visiting school for the first time. But why was Eliza breaking the rules?

Once we were out of Eliza's mother's sight, the twins ran ahead.

We walked a long way until we reached town. I could see the school ahead of us. But Eliza made a sudden turn before we reached it. We went down a busy, narrow street. Where were we going?

A minute later, Eliza stopped in front of a store. The sign in the window said PAWNSHOP: WE PAY CASH FOR VALUABLES.

Eliza opened the door and went inside.

Every space in the shop was filled. Banjos, pocket watches, clocks, rings, sleds, dishes, tools, and toys sat in a jumble. Dust floated in the air, and spiderwebs swayed in the corners. A grizzled man with brown-stained teeth sat behind the counter.

Let's get out of here, I begged Eliza.

She didn't listen.

She walked straight up to the man and showed me to him. "Mister, would you buy my doll?"

I gasped.

The man looked me over good. His searching eyes felt like bugs crawling on me. After a minute, he spat out of the side of his mouth. Gooey brown tobacco sailed into a bucket on the floor.

"I'll give you fifty cents for her," he said.

"Fifty cents? No fair!" said Eliza.

"Take it or leave it," said the man.

Eliza stomped back outside and away from the pawnshop.

I sighed with relief.

But then Eliza halted right in the middle of the sidewalk. She closed her eyes and took a deep breath. She turned, ran back inside the pawnshop, and told the man, "I'll take it."

The pawnshop owner opened a cash register. He held out his hand for me. He wouldn't give Eliza any money until she gave me up.

Eliza hugged me tight. "I'm sorry, Goldie. It's just

for a little while," she told me. "Pawnshops let you buy your stuff back, so I'll come back for you when we're rich again."

The man snorted. "Don't make promises you can't keep, girlie. None of us gonna be rich again anytime soon."

Eliza looked like she wanted to cry. She gave me one last hard, helpless hug. "You're my only friend. I love you, Goldie," she whispered.

I was too upset to answer.

Eliza took the ribbon from my hair when the pawnshop owner wasn't looking. She put it into her pocket.

Then she let me go.

CHAPTER 20
❖ Goldie's Story ❖
Wishing

*T*he awful man's fingers closed around me.

I heard the clink of coins as his money dropped into Eliza's hands.

Don't leave me here! I begged.

The door banged. Eliza left the pawnshop without me. Through the window, I watched her disappear down the sidewalk.

The pawnshop owner set me on a shelf.

The ticking of the clocks thundered in the silence of the shop. It sounded like Eliza's heartbeat when she'd held me close for the last time.

It wasn't fair. Just when Eliza had learned to love me, I'd lost her.

I wished, I wished! I wished for her with all my aching heart. My wishing grew and grew and grew.

Then something strange began to happen. I felt a

tingling in my toes. The tingles spread up my legs. They zapped throughout my body, quick as lightning.

Suddenly, I found myself floating in the air!

I looked down and saw my empty doll body on the pawnbroker's dusty shelf below me. But the invisible, inside part that is truly me floated away. I flew through the closed door as if it weren't even there. I was free!

I flew through the air. My doll body stayed behind. I didn't care.

I caught up with Eliza. She was crying.

I'm here! I told her.

She didn't hear me.

Eliza! I shouted.

Nothing. My girl couldn't hear me.

I followed her home.

"Why aren't you at school?" her mother asked when she saw Eliza. "What's wrong?"

Eliza couldn't speak. She gave the money to her mother.

"Where did you get this?" her mother asked in surprise.

"I s-s-sold Goldie," squeaked Eliza. "Is it enough to help buy back our old house?"

"Oh, honey. No, it's not. It —" began her mother.

Eliza didn't wait to hear more. She ran to her bedroom and flung herself on the bed.

Her mother came and sat beside her. She stroked

Eliza's hair. "I know how much you loved Goldie. It must have been hard for you to sell her. That was a brave thing you did to help the family. I'm proud of you."

Eliza just sobbed into her pillow.

The rest of the week passed, and Eliza's money didn't seem to change anything. "What happened to the money from Goldie?" she asked her mother one day.

"I gave it to your uncle to help pay our share of the electric bill," her mother answered.

"I traded Goldie for dumb old electricity?" asked Eliza.

"I use my electric sewing machine to earn money for our food," her mother told her. "You helped."

Eliza watched her sisters play with Ruby and Violet. "It wasn't worth it," she whispered.

The next morning, Eliza stopped outside the pawn-shop before school. She cupped her hands around her eyes and stared through the window. She looked every-where for the old me.

But I wasn't there anymore. I mean, my body wasn't. Eliza ran inside the shop.

"Where's Goldie?" she asked the pawnshop owner.

"Who?" he asked.

"My doll. She had on a green dress. I brought her in last week."

"Oh, yeah." The man shrugged. "Sold her."

CHAPTER 21
❖ Money ❖

*M*eooow! Ringo jumped into Far Nana's lap. George rubbed her ankles.

Far Nana stood up and stretched. "The cats need to be fed. Wait here. Be back in a jiff."

She stopped in the witch's hat doorway and turned back. "Unless you girls want to wait until tomorrow to hear the rest of Goldie's story . . . ?"

"No!" Rose and Lila said at the same time. "We'll wait for you."

All four cats followed Far Nana downstairs.

"I wonder what it felt like for Goldie to be floating around," Lila said once Far Nana was gone.

"I wonder what happened to Goldie's old body after she floated away," said Rose.

"Maybe it turned into a zombie," said Lila. "A Goldie zombie."

Rose thought of a joke. "Well, it couldn't have become a cheerleader doll."

"Why?"

"Because it had lost its spirit. Get it?" said Rose.

"Ha-ha," said Lila. "It's sad that Eliza sold Goldie, though."

"She had to. She needed money," said Rose. "Like us."

"I wish we had something we could sell," said Lila.

"Yeah," said Rose. "But most of our stuff is boxed up and stored while we stay at Far Nana's."

"Yeah. All we have are our lockets," said Lila.

Rose covered her locket with both hands. "No way!"

Lila covered hers, too. "Yeah. I'd rather eat slime and rockwiches forever than sell our lockets."

"We wouldn't need money if Mom and Dad had called," said Rose.

"I wonder why they didn't," said Lila. "Do you think something bad happened to them and Far Nana just isn't telling us?"

"No," said Rose. She wasn't sure, but she wanted to be brave for Lila. "They're probably just busy or their phones are broken or something. Help me think of a way to get some money just in case they can't call for a while."

They both stared into space, thinking of ways to earn money. Then Far Nana came back in.

"TBC," Rose said quickly. They both knew that meant To Be Continued.

Far Nana sat down again. "Sorry about that. Now where were we, Goldie? Oh, yes, back at the pawnshop."

CHAPTER 22
❧ Goldie's Story ❧
Riches to Rags

"You *sold* Goldie?" Eliza asked the pawnshop owner. "But I was going to buy her back."

"With what? You ain't got any money," said the man.

Eliza backed away from him until she bumped into the door. She ran all the way home. I followed with a heavy heart.

Eliza cried herself to sleep that night.

Her mother was too busy sewing to pay attention to her. Night and day, I heard the buzz of her sewing machine in the kitchen. I knew the family needed the money her sewing brought in. But couldn't her mother see Eliza needed her, too?

"Oh, Goldie," Eliza wailed into her pillow. "I miss you!" She rubbed my green hair ribbon against her cheek until it grew wet with her tears.

I miss you, too! I told her. She didn't hear me. I couldn't comfort my girl because she didn't know I was there.

I couldn't even share my troubles with Ruby and Violet. I had discovered they couldn't hear me, either. What good was a doll with no body? I was useless.

Later that night, I was watching Eliza sleep when I felt an odd tingling. It was the same tingling I'd felt before I'd left my old body back at the pawnshop. The tingles zapped through me.

A great force began tugging me away from my girl. I tried to fight it. But the force was unstoppable. I flew out of Eliza's room, down the hall, and into the kitchen.

I landed with a thud. Once I'd caught my breath, I looked down at myself.

I had become a new doll!

My skin was no longer slick and shiny. Now I was made of cloth. I was wearing a green-flowered dress. Burlap shoes peeked out from below the hem. I still had golden hair, only now it was made of yarn.

My long-ago wish had come true. I was a hand-made, one-of-a-kind rag doll. There wasn't another doll like me anywhere in the world.

Eliza's mother picked me up. She carried me down the hall and tucked me in bed beside Eliza.

I could hardly wait for my girl to wake up.

But would she still love me now that I was just a rag doll?

CHAPTER 23
❖ Goldie's Story ❖
A New Goldie

*I*s that you, Goldie? asked Ruby.

Where have you been? asked Violet. *We've been worried about you.*

I blinked at the other dolls as I awoke. They were sitting on the twins' empty beds. The twins were already up and gone.

How did you know it was me? I asked the dolls.

We could just tell, said Ruby.

What happened to you? Violet asked. *You look so different.*

I quickly explained. Ruby and Violet were glad to see me. Would Eliza be?

Eliza yawned, stretched, and slowly woke up. She stared at me in surprise. Then she reached out and smoothed my hair. "Where did you come from?" she asked softly.

"I made her for you," her mother replied from the bedroom doorway. She came inside and sat on the end of Eliza's bed. "To help make up for losing Goldie. I'm sorry there isn't enough money to buy you a new doll."

Eliza turned me around and around. "She's beautiful! How did you make her?"

Beautiful? Eliza thought I was beautiful!

"I made her body from a flour sack and her dress from a feed sack," explained her mother. She lifted my feet to show Eliza. "Her shoes were made out of a burlap potato sack. Your father brought the sacks and her sawdust stuffing from the farm. The thread for her eyes and mouth came from your sisters' old dresses. I made her hair from the tassels on my best yellow shawl."

So that's what her mother had been doing every night. She had been making a new me. She hadn't been ignoring Eliza at all.

"I've got something for my new doll, too," said Eliza. She pulled my old green ribbon from her pocket and tied it into a bow in my hair.

She leaned close to me. "Your hair is the same color as my Goldie's," she whispered. "You remind me of her. I think I'll call you Goldie, too."

Eliza hugged her mother. My soft body got squished between them. "Thank you for making a new Goldie for me. I love her."

My girl loved me! Even though I wasn't a shiny Happy Abby look-alike doll anymore. I was glad.

Still, I wondered what had happened to my former

doll body. Did it lie empty in another girl's house? Or had it become home to the spirit of some other doll? I would never know.

Over the following years, life was hard for us. But Eliza and I faced the tough times and good times together. And things did get better.

Eliza's father got a job at another bank. The family moved to a new house. It wasn't as big as their old one, but Eliza and I liked having our own room again.

I was with Eliza when she made a best friend in our new neighborhood.

When she got older, I went with her to college and listened to her giggle about boys.

Years later, I even went to her wedding. I sat in a chair on a white satin pillow and watched her walk down the aisle in a lace gown. Some of the guests stared at me, wondering why a rag doll was a wedding guest.

But I was happy in my one-of-a-kind body because my Eliza loved me. She loved me so much that she never bought another doll.

Even when I grew old and tattered, Eliza took good care of me. She didn't give me away. Because —

I was too special.

CHAPTER 24
❖ Now or Never ❖

Rose sighed dreamily. "I love happy endings."
"Me, too," said Far Nana.

"Me three," said Lila.

Ssst! Ssst! Far Nana steam ironed the wrinkles out of Goldie's clean, mended dress. She waved it around to cool it off. Then she slipped the dress back onto Goldie.

"She looks great!" said Lila.

"I'm glad you didn't make Goldie look too new," said Rose. "She still looks old, but way better than when she came."

"Old dolls have a special charm," said Far Nana. "I'm sure Mrs. Shaw wouldn't have wanted Goldie to lose that."

"I wonder how Mrs. Shaw got Goldie?" asked Rose.

"We'll have to ask Goldie later," said Far Nana. "But now it's time to hit the sack."

"Why do you say 'go to bed' that way?" asked Lila.

"It's just a saying. Slang," said Far Nana.

"Like when you said computers and TV aren't your bag?" asked Lila.

"Right," said Far Nana. "Or like saying *swell* or *ducky* to mean *good*. Those were slang words people used during the Great Depression."

"Why did they call it the Great Depression?" asked Rose. "There was nothing great about it."

"Yeah," said Lila. "They should have called it the Not-So-Great Depression."

"*Great* doesn't always mean *good*. It also means *big*. The Depression years were a big change for everyone who lost money," said Far Nana.

Money? Rose took a deep breath. It was now or never. "Speaking of money, do you have any to spare? We need to buy lunch and stuff for school."

"We were going to ask Mom and Dad," Lila added. "But they didn't call."

Rose hurried on. "And we need school supplies fast. We know you're kind of poor. So you don't have to give us any allowance or anything."

"Poor?" Far Nana looked surprised. "What makes you think I'm poor?"

"Because you shop at garage sales and you write lists on old envelopes," said Rose.

"Plus you eat weeds," said Lila. "And you have a ton of bills."

Far Nana chuckled. "I see where you got the idea.

But I'm not poor. I'm just thrifty. I can pay all the bills and buy the things you need, too."

"Including a computer and TV?" asked Rose.

Far Nana smiled but shook her head. "I said *need*. Not *want*."

CHAPTER 25
❦ The Gift ❦

As they were walking home from school the next day, Rose had an idea.

"Here's the next hard question," she told Lila. "And it's your turn to ask Far Nana."

"What?"

"Ask her how she talks to dolls."

"Maybe," said Lila. "I'll think about it."

When they got home, Rose and Lila ran upstairs and found Far Nana in the witch's hat. Goldie wasn't in her usual place on the pillow. Instead, a picture of her after she was all finished lay there.

"Where's Goldie?" Rose asked.

"Mrs. Shaw picked her up today," said Far Nana.

"Rats," said Lila. "Another doggone doll gone."

"But — did Mrs. Shaw tell you how she got Goldie?" asked Rose.

"No, and I didn't get a chance to talk to Goldie again before she left," said Far Nana.

"Far Nana?" Lila asked. "How do you talk to dolls, anyway?"

Far Nana thought for a minute. Then she said, "It's a gift. All old dolls have stories. You simply have to learn to listen."

Rose liked the way Far Nana talked to Lila and her like they were grown-ups. She didn't say things like "You'll understand when you're older."

"If it's so easy, why can't everyone do it?" asked Rose.

"I didn't say it was easy," said Far Nana.

"Can you teach us?" asked Lila.

"It's not something just anyone can learn. You have to have the gift," said Far Nana.

"How do we know if we have it?" asked Rose.

"When you hold a doll, try to imagine its life before you met it," said Far Nana. "It won't work the first time. You have to keep trying."

"Can Mom do it?" asked Lila.

"You'll have to ask her," said Far Nana.

Ding-dong! The doorbell rang. Rose and Lila raced downstairs, with Far Nana close behind.

When they opened the front door, there was a box on the porch. A delivery truck was zooming away.

Lila read the box's label. "It's from Mom and Dad! It says super speedy delivery, so it must be super important."

Far Nana pulled the box inside and opened it.

Lila grabbed handfuls of mushy white Styrofoam peanuts from the box and tossed them into the air. "They sent us ghost poo!"

The cats batted the packing peanuts around until Far Nana shooed them away.

Underneath the peanuts, the girls found some African-looking stuff. And two notes. One for Rose and Lila. And one for Far Nana.

Rose read their note aloud:

"Dear Rose and Lila,
    Some of the African villagers made these gifts for you. We hope you enjoy them.
    We can't call you this week because we'll be working in a really small village that doesn't have phones. We'll call next week, as always.
                We love you,
                Mom and Dad"

"So that's why they didn't call," said Rose.

Lila dug deeper in the box. "Look at this cool stuff." She pulled out a painted wooden thing that looked like a bowling pin. It made musical sounds when she shook it. Next came a flat wooden board with ten round cups carved into its top and a bag of small stones.

"I think that's an African game called Oware," said

Far Nana. "My note from your parents says they'll tell us how to play it next time they call."

Lila kept digging. She found two objects that looked like carved chess pieces with hair. "Little dolls!" She gave one to Rose.

Rose held the doll with both hands and stared at it. She tried to imagine its life before she met it. Nothing.

At the bottom of the box, Lila found a bunch of colorful bands and clips. She handed them to Rose.

"Hair stuff!" Rose headed upstairs. "I'm going to go try some of it on."

"We're going shopping this afternoon. Be ready in fifteen minutes," Far Nana called after her.

"Okay!" Rose called back. Up in her bedroom, she gathered her hair into a ponytail with an African clip. She divided the ponytail into a bunch of little braids with smaller clips on the ends.

"Time to go!" Far Nana called up the stairs a bit later.

"Coming!" Rose started to run out the bedroom door. She stopped and stared at herself in the mirror. She looked really different. If Nadia saw her, would she laugh? If Bart saw her, would he tease her? Maybe she should take her hair down.

"Rose?" called Far Nana.

Rose headed downstairs and outside with her hair still in braids.

Far Nana was on the porch, jangling her keys. In the driveway, Lila was sitting in the van with the door open. She was making noisy music with the African bowling pin.

Next-door Nadia was in her yard. She waved at Rose. "I like your hair!" she shouted.

Rose smiled and waved back. "Thanks!" She skipped after Far Nana to the rainbow van and hopped in the backseat.

Sometimes being different was kind of cool.

CHAPTER 26
❖ Eliza ❖

When they got back from shopping, there was a note in the mailbox.

Lila pulled it out and then handed it to Far Nana. "It's for you."

Rose and Lila looked over Far Nana's arm as she read:

"*Dear Doll Doctor,*
Goldie looks wonderful!
She is so special to me.
Thank you for making her well.
Best wishes,
Mrs. Elizabeth W. Shaw'"

Rose gasped. "Look how she signed it: Elizabeth. I bet Eliza is short for Elizabeth."

"So Mrs. Shaw is Eliza all grown up," said Lila. "Cool!"

They took their packages inside, and Far Nana went into the kitchen to fix dinner.

Rose and Lila set the table. Then they put away their packages.

Lila kept out one notebook she had bought. It came with a magnet and had a big cartoon dog on the front. The dog was covered with a sheet of plastic that had black metal shavings inside. She used the magnet to draw a metal shavings beard on the dog's face. Then she shook the notebook, and the beard went away.

Rose's favorite new thing was a key chain that clipped onto her backpack. She had bought a pink-haired troll doll charm for it, and she could add more things later.

After a while, Rose flopped on the couch in the living room. "I guess Mom and Dad aren't calling until next week. So we're going to be bored tonight."

"Let's play a b-o-r-e-d game then. I'll pick one out." Lila dug in the closet for a minute. "Bingo!"

"No bingo," said Rose. "I hate that game."

"Not really bingo," said Lila. "I meant 'Bingo—I found a game.' And it's perfect for you." She whipped the game from behind her back and showed it to Rose. "Ta-da! S-*crab*-ble!"

Rose gave Lila The Eye. "Since I like it, I'll play it. But I'm *not* crabby anymore."

"You sound crabby," said Lila.

"Well, I'm not. But if you don't cut it out, that might change any minute."

Before Lila could say anything, Far Nana called them for dinner. "Hope you girls like seafood."

"Sure," said Lila. "We're on a seafood diet. Right, Rose?"

"We *see* food, and we eat it," Rose and Lila said together.

Far Nana laughed. "That's good. Because tonight's dinner is crab salad."

Rose groaned.

Lila giggled so hard she fell over.

Far Nana looked confused. "What?"

"Never mind," said Rose. "Let's eat."

Glossary

bisque   porcelain that is not very shiny

Black Tuesday   October 29, 1929, the day the stock market of the United States crashed. This was the start of the Great Depression.

ceramic   materials such as clay that are used to make dolls and pottery

china   shiny porcelain

composition doll   a type of doll made between 1900 and 1950 from a mixture of paper, wood pulp, sawdust, and glue. The mixture was pressed into molds to shape the doll's head and body. After the molded head and body dried, they were painted and varnished so they became shiny. Dolls made of composition were not as breakable as bisque and china dolls. When plastic was invented, it replaced composition for doll-making because plastic lasted longer.

demand   a need for goods or services

economy   a financial system

foreclose   a legal way to take property from an owner who doesn't make payments

the Great Depression   a financial crisis in the United States that lasted from 1929 to 1939

investor   a person who buys stock in a company

kiln   a special oven used for baking ceramic and porcelain at very hot temperatures

mohair   a type of doll's hair made from the coat of an Angora goat

porcelain   a fine-grained ceramic material that is heated in a kiln and is breakable

rumble seat   a small passenger seat at the back end of some 1920s cars

stock market   a system in which people buy and sell stocks

stocks   shares of ownership in a company

Questions and Answers About the Great Depression

What caused the Great Depression?
In the United States, the stock market crashed on October 29, 1929. That day became known as Black Tuesday. It was the beginning of the Great Depression.

Most people didn't know how bad the economy in the United States had become by 1929. That's because businesses had sold lots of products and made money in the early 1920s.

Many Americans had invested in businesses by buying shares called stock in the companies. Some of them bought stocks using credit. This means they borrowed money to buy the stocks. They thought their stocks would soon be worth more money. They planned to sell their stocks and make a profit.

Many companies and investors got rich in the 1920s. But not all workers were paid well. Soon, workers couldn't afford to buy the things that businesses made. Because there was less demand, businesses made fewer products. They didn't need as many workers, so a number of workers lost their jobs.

Companies stopped growing, and their stocks were soon worth less money. So people who had bought stocks on credit couldn't pay for them.

On Black Tuesday, investors suddenly panicked. They sold stocks as fast as they could. They even sold stocks for less than they originally paid for them.

This started a cycle that hurt the economy of the United States. Many banks and businesses closed. People lost their jobs and could not find new ones.

Was everyone poor during the Great Depression?
Some families in the United States did not suffer during the Great Depression. But most did.

People had to do without everyday things like toothpaste, toilet paper, and soft drinks. They could not even buy enough food. Some people had to comb their hair with a fork because they didn't even have two cents to buy a comb.

Many families lost their homes because they couldn't make the monthly payments. Hundreds of homeless families lived in tents or shacks grouped together on empty land. These areas became known as tent cities. Some people blamed President Herbert Hoover for not fixing the problems of the Depression. They called the tent cities "Hoovervilles."

During the Great Depression, everyone in the family tried to earn money or help out somehow. Most women did not have jobs outside the home in those days. They sewed, baked, or cleaned homes for other families who could pay them.

Children did household chores such as washing clothes, cleaning, and cooking. Some of them even worked at jobs in factories or other businesses.

Men who had lost their jobs went out looking for work every day. But most of them couldn't find jobs, no matter how hard they tried.

Many schools didn't have money to buy books for students during the Great Depression. Sometimes children couldn't go to school because their clothes were too worn-out. If children wore holes in the bottoms of their shoes, their parents couldn't buy them a new pair. So, they put a piece of cardboard inside the bottom of their old shoes and kept wearing them. Some children traded off days when they would wear the family's only good clothes or shoes to school. Other families were so poor that children had to trade off days eating lunch!

Charities helped by giving away food in soup kitchens. Hundreds of people stood in long lines called *bread lines*, waiting for their turn to get free food.

Most people wanted to work and earn money. They were not used to being poor. They were embarrassed. They didn't want to accept charity unless they had to.

What did children do for fun during the Great Depression?

Children and their families found ways to have fun during the Great Depression. They did things that were free. They read library books or played in the park or at the beach. Children made their own toys, such as scootermobiles. They played simple games including checkers, cards, marbles, hopscotch, jacks, and jump rope. Boys played baseball, but not many girls did.

The game Monopoly was invented in 1932, during the Great Depression. Since they didn't have enough real money, people thought it was fun to play a game with pretend money.

Few families had TV in those days, but many listened to the radio. The whole family would gather around the radio at night. They listened to music, news, comedy shows, and adventure shows.

Adventure comics became popular during the Great Depression. Tarzan, Superman, and Little Orphan Annie comics were all created in the 1930s.

People went to the movies if they could afford to pay a nickel or dime for a ticket. Movies made in the 1930s include *King Kong*, *Dracula*, and Walt Disney's *Snow White and the Seven Dwarfs*.

How did the Great Depression change people?

People who grew up during the Great Depression remember what it was like to be poor. Today, many of them are careful about spending money. They know how to save things and reuse them.

During the Depression, people often made their own clothes. Flour was sold in large white sacks in the 1930s. After the flour was used, the empty sacks were reused to make children's underclothes. Chicken feed was sold in brightly colored, flowered sacks. Those empty sacks were cleaned and reused to make dresses.

What ended the Great Depression?
The Great Depression lasted about ten years, from 1929 to 1939. When Franklin D. Roosevelt became President in 1933, more than thirteen million people were jobless. They were scared. President Roosevelt made a speech to try to calm everyone. He said something that became famous: "The only thing we have to fear is fear itself."

President Roosevelt created government programs that put people back to work. The Works Progress Administration (WPA) created many new jobs. WPA workers built bridges, roads, and dams, including the Hoover Dam in Nevada. The Civilian Conservation Corps (CCC) provided jobs for men ages eighteen to twenty-five. They planted trees and built roads in the forest.

Before the Great Depression, if a bank went out of business and your money was in that bank, you would often lose all of your money. President Roosevelt made new rules for banks. He promised people that money they put in banks would be safer from then on.

President Franklin D. Roosevelt helped lead the United States out of the Great Depression.

How much did things cost during the Great Depression?

dress	$2.00
sweater	$1.00
coat	$7.00
shoes	$2.00
bread	19 cents
milk	15 cents
soft drink	5 cents
movie ticket	5 or 10 cents
movie popcorn	5 cents
haircut	20 cents
doll	$1.50
bike	$11.00
basketball	$1.00
baseball glove and ball	$1.25
car	$600.00–$1,000.00
house	$3,000.00

Slang Words Used in the Great Depression	What the Words Meant
a good egg	a popular person
all wet	not good
And how!	I agree!
boffo; clam; lizard; buck	one dollar
dogs	feet
dolled up	dressed up
five spot; Lincoln	five-dollar bill
gams; stilts	legs
Hot diggity dawg!	How great!
lift it	move over
marble palace; poet's corner; Egypt	toilet
Nerts!	I'm amazed!
oodles	a lot of something
snazzy; ducky; swell; swanky	very good
suds; bacon; dough; bread; cabbage	money
Tin Lizzie; tin can	car
yowsah; yo; pos-o-lute-ly	yes

Watch for the third book in the
✚ **Doll Hospital** ✚ series,

Glory's Freedom:
A STORY OF THE UNDERGROUND RAILROAD,
coming soon.

In Doll Hospital #3: *Glory's Freedom: A Story of the Underground Railroad,* Rose and Lila go to a doll auction with Far Nana . . .

"See this?" Far Nana shined her flashlight against the side of a bisque doll's head. Rose and Lila leaned closer.

"There's a crack!" said Rose.

When the light was on you could see a long crack in the doll's pretty face. When it was off, you couldn't.

"This doll has been repaired. Good job, too. I couldn't have done it better myself," said Far Nana as she set the doll back down.

A brown-skinned woman with long black beaded braids and a camera around her neck was standing next to them.

"Do you repair dolls?" she asked Far Nana.

"Yes, I run a doll hospital," said Far Nana.

"My name is Andrea Tate," the woman told them. "Last week, my husband and I found an old doll in our basement. I'm taking it to the auctioneer now for today's sale."

The woman set the box she was holding on a table, opened it, and pulled out a doll.

Far Nana put a hand over her heart. "Oh! She's lovely!"

Rose and Lila gave each other sideways looks. The doll's black hair was tangled and its poofy skirt was stained and torn. The ribbons holding its straw bonnet were gone. There were tiny cracks all over its arms and legs. Worst of all, its nose was missing.

But as usual, thought Rose, Far Nana saw beyond what a doll looked like on the outside. She could see way down to its beauty underneath.

"It looks sort of like a candle," said Rose.

"Or like Far Nana's beauty soap," said Lila.

Mrs. Tate held her doll away from Rose and Lila as though she didn't want them to touch it.

"It's made of wax. Very delicate," warned the woman.

"Hint, hint," Rose whispered to Lila. "She means that she doesn't want kids like us anywhere near her doll."

"As if we would hurt it!" Lila whispered back.

"The auctioneer told us to repair the doll before we tried to sell it," Mrs. Tate went on. "But since we couldn't find anyone to work on it, we decided to put it on the auction today as it is. If it doesn't sell, are you interested in repairing it?"

"I'd love to work on such a beautiful doll," said Far Nana. "What's its finding story?"

"Finding story? I don't understand," said Mrs. Tate.

"That's what we doll people call the story of how you found the doll or where it came from."

Mrs. Tate's voice got excited. "I'm a photographer and I'm having the basement of my house remodeled to become my office. When the construction crew began work, we found this doll hidden in the wall. We have no idea how long she'd been there or how she got there. Too bad she can't tell us."

Rose and Lila looked at each other. Yeah, too bad, they said in silent sister brain wave talk.

Joan Holub